A DINO **EASY** READER

Rex and Lilly
Schooltime

Stories by Laurie Krasny Brown

Pictures by Marc Brown

Little, Brown and Company

Boston   New York   London

*Special thanks to Andrea Powning of the Derby School
in Hingham, Massachusetts, and to Laurel S. Ernst of the
Chappaqua School District, in Chappaqua, New York.*

First Paperback Edition

A Dino Easy Reader and the Dinosaur logo
are trademarks of Little, Brown and Company.

Library of Congress Cataloging-in-Publication Data

Brown, Laurene Krasny.
    Rex and Lilly schooltime / stories by Laurie Krasny Brown ;
pictures by Marc Brown. — 1st ed.
        p.   cm. — (A Dino easy reader)
    Summary: Dinosaur siblings Rex and Lilly have a busy day in school
taking part in show-and-tell, trading lunches, and reading.
    ISBN 0-316-10920-7 (hc) / ISBN 0-316-13535-6 (pb)
    [1. Schools — Fiction. 2. Brothers and sisters — Fiction.
3. Dinosaurs — Fiction.] I. Brown, Marc Tolon, ill. II. Title.
III. Series: Brown, Laurene Krasny. Dino easy reader.
PZ7.B816114Rdk   1997
[E] — dc20   95-2912
                    HC: 10 9 8 7 6 5 4 3
                    PB: 10 9 8 7 6 5 4 3 2 1
                                LAKE

Printed in the United States of America

Contents

Show-and-Tell 4

Want to Trade? 11

Lilly Reads 23

Show-and-Tell

"Who is ready for show-and-tell?"

asked Mr. B.

"Okay, Rex! You may go first."

"My show-and-tell is a secret,"

said Rex.

"Give us a clue!" said Alex.

"Okay," said Rex.

"It's a secret,

but it's one we all have."

"Is it your journal?" asked Amy.

"Nope!" said Rex.

"It isn't my journal."

"Give us a new clue," said Nora.

"Okay," said Rex.

"It's right here,

but you can't see it."

"Is it in your pocket?" asked Ned.

"Nope!" said Rex.

"It's not in my pocket.

Okay, one last clue.

Where I go, it goes."

"Is it your belly button?"

asked Amos.

Want to Trade?

"Time for lunch!" said Mr. B.

"Yippee!" said the kids.

"Yuck!" said Rex.

"Look at this yucky lunch!

This lunch is too yucky to eat."

"Want to trade?"

Rex asked Amos.

"I can eat your lunch.

And you can eat mine."

"All right!" said Amos.

Then Amos saw Amy's lunch.

Her lunch looked better.

Amos said, "Amy, will you

trade lunch with me?"

"Okay, but I want to

keep my treats," said Amy.

"No fair!" said Amos.

But the rest looked good.

"Well, okay!" said Amos.

So Amos traded lunch with Amy.

Then Millie saw Amy's new lunch.

"Mmm," said Millie.

"I like your new lunch, Amy.

Want to trade?"

"I want my treats," said Amy.

"But I'll trade the rest."

"Trade just one treat?"

asked Millie. "Look, *I* have chips!"

"Yes!" said Amy.

"Max—stop!" said Millie.

"Don't eat that cookie!"

Max stopped.

"Why not?" he asked.

"Let's trade lunch!"

   said Millie.

"Want to?"

"Okay!" said Max.

   So they traded lunch, too.

Then Max saw Rex's lunch.

"Rex," he said,

"will you trade lunch with me?

What do you say?"

"I say yes!" said Rex.

"Let's trade!"

By now Rex was really ready for lunch!

"Here goes!" he said.

Rex took a bite of lunch.

"Yum! This is yummy!" he said.

"What is this?"

Rex took a good look.

"Hey, this is *my* lunch!"

he said.

"And it's great!"

"Lilly," said Mrs. Woo,

"please read the next page out loud.

Page six."

Lilly looked at page six.

She read,

"Long, long ago

in a far-off land,

there lived an elf

who was a bit of a..."

Lilly stopped.

"Very good, Lilly," said Mrs. Woo.

"Please go on."

Lilly looked at page six.

"I can't go on!" she said.

"I can't read the next word. It's too—"

"I can! I can!" Willy called out.

"But Willy," said Mrs. Woo.

"It's Lilly's turn.

 You can read this word, Lilly,"

she said.

"You can sound it out."

"It's too hard!" said Lilly.

Willy called out again,

"I can sound it out!

I can sound out this word."

"But Willy, it's still Lilly's turn,"

said Mrs. Woo.

"Lilly, just try!"

So Lilly said the sounds out loud:

"P

E."

"It's a short *e,* as in *elf,*" said Mrs. Woo.

"S

T."

"Now say them again,"

said Mrs. Woo.

Lilly said them again.

"*P-e-s-t.*"

And again.

She said them faster.

And faster.

All of a sudden Lilly stopped

and looked at page six.

Then she read right out loud:

"Long, long ago

in a far-off land,

there lived an elf

who was a bit of a...

pest!"

"Yes!" said Mrs. Woo.

"Good work, Lilly!"

"And Willy," said Lilly,

"that goes for you, too.

You are a bit of a pest!"

Then Lilly read

and read

and read.